A St
in Small Town

award

Small Town was a happy place with lots of happy people.

So, when the town crier cried out, "Farmer Soil's carrots have been taken!" everyone was shocked.

This had never happened before in Small Town.

Everyone gathered in the town square. Where could Farmer Soil's carrots have gone?

Just then, a little girl pointed at a boy in the large crowd.

"I have never seen him before," she said. The people didn't know him. He was a stranger.

All the people of the town looked at the stranger. He had a very sad face.

"I'm sorry. I have nowhere to live and I was so hungry. I didn't know what to do," he said. "I took Farmer Soil's carrots." His head dropped.

The people didn't know what to say. They felt sorry for the stranger.

"What is your name?" asked Mr Cloak crossly.

"Oakley," replied the boy.

"You must not take things that are not yours," said Mr Cloak with a stern face. "You must leave Small Town!"

Oakley knew he had done a bad thing and he was not welcome there.

"My goodness," said Mrs Joiner. "That was very mean," she told Farmer Soil unhappily.

"But the boy stole my carrots," said Farmer Soil crossly.

"I know, but he didn't have a choice. He was starving," said Mrs Joiner.

She was right. This made Farmer Soil feel very bad.

Farmer Soil and Mrs
Joiner went together to
talk to Mr Cloak.

They told him that his
treatment of Oakley had
been too harsh.

Mr Cloak felt bad.
"I know you are right.
We should help the boy,"
he said.

So Mrs Joiner told
Farmer Soil and Mr Cloak
that she had a plan.

They all agreed it was
a very good plan, and
they went to find Oakley.

They looked for him everywhere, but he was nowhere to be seen.

"He has gone, but I know where he went," said the same little girl as before.

"I will go after him and ask him to come back," said Farmer Soil.

The people of Small Town cheered.

Luckily, Oakley had not gone far at all.

"Oakley!" called Farmer Soil. The boy turned as the farmer ran up to him. "You need to come back," he puffed. "We have a plan you need to hear," he said.

He took Oakley to see Mrs Joiner at Mr Cloak's clock shop. They told him the plan before telling the rest of the town.

Back in the town, Oakley stood still as Mrs Joiner told everyone their plan.

Oakley did not know if they would agree. His knees knocked as he waited.

The plan was this: Oakley was to live with Mrs Joiner, and Mr Cloak would give him a job in the clock shop.

Everyone was thrilled and cheered loudly.

Oakley was so happy that he hopped up and down with joy.

Oakley has lived in Small Town ever since. He likes living with Mrs Joiner and works hard at the clock shop with Mr Cloak.

What a kind and happy place Small Town was after all!

Oakley

Do you think Oakley was right to take the carrots?

clock

Who owned the clock shop?

Mrs Joiner

Describe Mrs Joiner's character.

Farmer Soil

What did Farmer Soil do to show he'd forgiven Oakley?

Small Town

What do you think was happening in the town on the day Oakley arrived?

everyone

How do you think everyone felt about the plan?

Notes for Parents and Teachers

Popular Rewards Early Readers have been specially created to build young readers' vocabulary, develop their comprehension skills and boost their progress towards independent reading.

★ Make reading fun. Why not read the story and have your child clap when they hear a featured phonics sound, then race to find it on the page?

★ Encourage your child to read aloud to help pick up and resolve any difficulties. As their skills grow, it will also help their fluency and expression.

★ The list of phonics sounds and 'tough and tricky' words will help to consolidate their learning.

★ Read and answer the questions together to develop comprehension and communication skills.

★ Always keep a positive attitude and focus on your child's achievements. This will help their confidence and build their enjoyment of reading.

ISBN 978-1-78270-616-8
Illustrated by Chris Rothero
Copyright © Award Publications Limited
Popular Rewards® is a registered trademark of Award Publications Limited
This edition first published 2023
Published by Award Publications Limited,
The Old Riding School, Welbeck, Worksop, S80 3LR
 /awardpublications @award.books @award_books
www.awardpublications.co.uk
23-1055 1
Printed in China